Leila's Magical Monster Party

Leila is determined to
have a party – even
though she is in bed
with a broken leg. But
her guests are not the
usual kind of guests –
they are the real
baddies!

Other books by Ann Jungman

There's a Troll at the Bottom
     of my Garden *(and sequels)*
     Puffin

Vlad the Drac *(and sequels)*
     Harper Collins

Sasha and the Wolfcub
Sasha and the Wolfchild
     Harper Collins

Broomstick Services
Broomstick Removals
Broomstick Rescues
Broomstick Babe
School for Dragons
     Scholastic

Frank N. Stein Books
     Orchard

Dracula is Backula
     Andersen

Ann Jungman

Leila's Magical Monster Party

Illustrated by Doffy Weir

BARN OWL BOOKS

First published in Great Britain 1991
by Viking Penguin Books Ltd
27 Wrights Lane, London W8 5TZ
This edition first published 2000
by Barn Owl Books
15 New Cavendish Street
London W1M 7RL
Barn Owl Books are distributed by
Frances Lincoln

Text copyright © 1991, 2000
Ann Jungman
Illustrations copyright © 1991, 2000
Doffy Weir

ISBN 1 903015 05 7

A CIP catalogue record for this book
is available from the British Library

Designed and typeset by Douglas Martin
Printed and bound in Great Britain
by Cox & Wyman Limited, Reading

Contents

Invitations

Leila was bored. She was very, very bored. A month ago, she had broken her leg and she was *still* stuck in bed. At first, in the hospital, it had been fun. There had been lots and lots of visitors and the other children to play with, but now she was back at home in her own bedroom.

Most days, Dad went off to work and her sister Louise went to school. Mum had taken time off work, but each day she had to go out and do the shopping and the rest of the time she was usually busy. There was no one else to play with or talk to.

Leila watched TV a lot, but even *that* got boring after a while. People kept bringing Leila books, but she had already read them. She had been given a book of fairy stories though, and they were very good. They were so good that she read them through twice.

"Nice to see you so involved in a book," said Leila's dad.

"I really like these stories," she told him. "There are so many baddies in them and they are so very, very bad!"

Her father laughed. "So you like the baddies do you?"

"Yes. The worse they are, the better I like them, but they're not as good as having someone to talk to. I can't react *all* the time. Oh, Dad, I'm so bored."

"Tell you what," said Dad. "I'll move your bed over by the window, then you can look out and see what's going on."

"Nothing goes on out there," muttered Leila. "It's just the backs of houses and gardens."

But she let her father move her bed and she opened the window and began to feed the birds some old bread.

"I wish I could get up and go and play in the garden," said Leila to herself. Just then, Mum opened the door. She was carrying a tray with a glass of milk and some biscuits and a letter addressed to Leila.

"Here's a letter for you," said
Mum, handing her the envelope.
Leila tore it open and there was an
invitation to a party.

Joanne Morris invites
Leila
to her party on Saturday
at 3 p.m.
RSVP

Leila burst into tears.

"It's not fair! I can't go! I'm fed
up! Why did I have to break
my leg?"

Mum gave her a big hug and tried to make her feel better.

"Come on love, it isn't for much longer. As soon as that horrible old plaster is off you can give a party and invite all your friends."

"I don't want to wait until then," said Leila. "I want to give a party today."

"Not today," said her mother. "That's much too soon. Why don't you make a list of who you want to invite? You can then draw some nice invitation cards and we can address them and send them out."

So Leila began to write a list.

17

"I'm *not* going to wait until my leg is better," she thought. "I shall give my party this afternoon. I'm going to invite all the people who never usually get invited to a party." And Leila began to write:

The Wolf from
Little Red Riding Hood
The Dragon from
St George and the Dragon
The Forty Thieves from
Ali Baba and the Forty Thieves
The Ugly Sisters from
Cinderella
The Giant from
Jack and the Beanstalk

19

"They'll be so pleased to be invited," said Leila, smiling to herself. She reached for her crayons and began to make invitations for all the people on her list.

"I'll make them just like the one that was sent to me this morning," she thought.

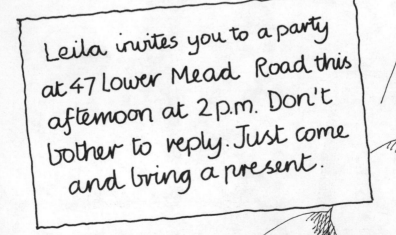

Leila invites you to a party at 47 Lower Mead Road this afternoon at 2 p.m. Don't bother to reply. Just come and bring a present.

When Mum came back, Leila said, firmly, "I *am* going to give a party."

"Don't be silly darling," replied her mum. "Your plaster isn't off yet and all your friends are at school."

"I know, but I'm not going to invite my usual friends. I'm going to invite all my favourite characters from the fairy stories."

"Oh, I see," said her mother, looking relieved. "*That* sort of a party."

"Yes, *that* sort of a party," agreed Leila. "So we need lots of food. I've invited so many guests and I expect they'll be very hungry."

"What do you want?" asked her mother.

"Sausages on sticks, and crisps and cheese and pineapple cubes, and lots and lots of cakes."

"All right," said her mother.
Half an hour later, Mum returned
with a tray full of nice things still
in their packets.

"That's not nearly enough,"
said Leila. "I've got lots of guests
coming and dragons and wolves
and giants have big appetites.

"Well it will have to do," said her mother. "I'm going shopping, but Dad's downstairs. I won't be long. You have a little sleep.

Mum gave her a kiss and went out. Leila heard the front door slam.

"Sleep indeed," said Leila, smiling to herself. "How can I sleep when I've got so many important guests coming to my party?"

The Party

On the dot of 2 p.m. Leila saw
her door open slowly. A wolf's
nose came round the door.

"Are you Leila?" asked the wolf.

"Yes," said Leila.

"I've come to the party," said
the wolf.

"Come on in," said Leila.
"You're the first to arrive."

"I usually am," said the wolf. "Here's your present."

"Can I open it now?" asked Leila.

"Go ahead," said the wolf.

Leila opened the parcel slowly. She cut the string and folded back the paper. There inside were a pair

of granny glasses.

"I don't wear glasses," said Leila.

"Well, I can't help that," said
the wolf. "I only got the invitation
a few minutes ago. It was all I
had left."

At that moment, the door was flung open and there stood a young man in a turban and behind him a whole row of others dressed just the same. The first young man bowed low to Leila.

"Greetings to you, O beautiful one," he said. "Please take this present, because my thirty-nine friends and I are all so happy to be invited to a party."

"You must be the forty thieves from *Ali Baba*," said Leila. "Come on in."

31

Leila opened her present. It was a beautiful diamond tiara.

"Oh," she gasped. "I've never seen anything so beautiful. Where did you get it?"

"Ask no questions and you'll get told no lies," said one of the

thieves, and they all giggled.

"It's stolen, isn't it?" said Leila.

"Course it is," said the thieves.
"What do you expect? Go on, put
it on."

So Leila put the tiara on and sat
up in bed feeling very important.
Then she heard the sound of loud
voices on the stairs.

"*I'm* going in first. Get out of my way, you skinny bean."

"No way," said another voice. "*I'm* going in first, you big potato."

Leila, the wolf and the forty thieves all looked hard at the door. In came two women, huffing and puffing, one long and skinny and the other short and fat.

"Hah," said the wolf. "It's the ugly sisters. I didn't know that you had invited *them*."

35

"We wouldn't have come if we'd known *you* were going to be here," said the two sisters as they walked over to Leila's bed. "Here's your present, dear. We hope you like it."

Leila was having a *wonderful* time. All these presents and just for her.

Carefully, she opened the
present the ugly sisters had given
her wrapped up in a newspaper.
Out fell a dusty slipper. Leila
found it difficult not to look
disappointed.

"What use is one old slipper?"
she asked.

"It's not any old slipper," said
the thin ugly sister.

"Just rub the dust off a bit," said
the fat ugly sister.

Leila did, and there, underneath,
was a glass slipper.

"It's the one Cinderella left at the ball," they told her.

"Once she married the prince she didn't worry about it. It's been under the bed ever since gathering dust, so we thought we'd bring it along."

"It's very pretty," said Leila. "But what can I use it for?"

"You could use it as a vase," said the fat sister.

"Or you could use it to keep things in," said the skinny sister.

Suddenly the house began to shake in a very frightening way.

"Whatever is happening?" said Leila, feeling scared.

The ugly sisters looked bad-tempered.

"Oh, no! Don't say you've gone and invited that silly old giant out of *Jack and the Beanstalk*?"

"Well, yes – I have," Leila told them.

"Boring!" yelled all the others.

The room got dark and Leila looked up to see a huge face with a bushy beard looking in through her window. She covered her eyes and screamed.

"Well," said the voice from outside. "That's a nice welcome I must say. Invited to a party and all I get is screams. I'll just take my present and go home."

"No, no!" cried Leila. "I'm sorry. Oh, please don't go. You just surprised me, that's all."

"I don't understand that," said the giant, sitting down on the lawn so that some light could come in. "After all, I *was* invited, but if it's any trouble I'll go home."

"No, do stay," said Leila.
"Did you say something about
a present?"

"Just a mo," said the giant,
and he put a giant hand into his
giant pocket. "There you are,"
he said, and handed her
a bean.

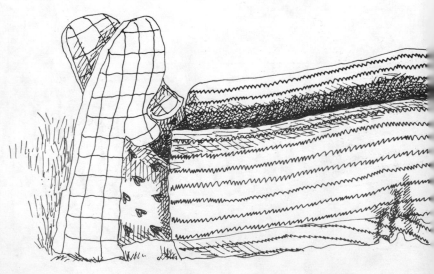

"It's a bean," said Leila. "What use is a bean?"

"That's just what Jack's mum said," said the giant. "And they did pretty well out of that bean, I can tell you!"

"Well," said Leila. "Thank you all for your lovely presents. I suppose we'd better play a game and then have tea."

Everyone thought that that was a good idea, so they started to play Pass the Parcel. The giant, who was too big to come inside the house, began to cry because he felt he was being left out, so they passed the parcel to him through the open window. They were having a great time, when suddenly it got very hot.

"Well, bless me," said the giant. "If it isn't the dragon from *St George and the Dragon*. Hello, dragon."

"Hello," said the dragon. "Sorry I'm late. Oh, you're in the middle of a game. Can I play too?

'Of course you can," said Leila.

"I'll stay out here with the giant," said the dragon. "Might be a bit dangerous if come into the house, if you know what I mean!"

"Quite," said Leila. "Did you remember a present?"

"Certainly," said the dragon. "I was very well brought up you know." He gave her a white sheet with a big red cross on it.

"An old sheet," said the giant. "What use is that?" He laughed

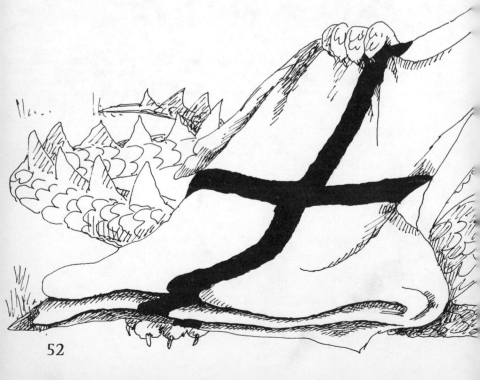

loudly and the others joined in.

"I think you are all very rude,"
said the dragon. "St George was

wearing that sheet the day we
had our fight. I took it off him and
from what I hear the Red Cross
now means a place where sick
people are being looked after."

"That's right," said Leila.

"Well then," said the dragon. "It will come in very useful. You're lying ill in bed, so we can put it on the roof and all the planes flying in the sky will know that someone here is ill. Come on, giant, help me put it on the roof."

So they put the sheet on the roof and went on playing Pass the Parcel. Then finally it was time for tea.

Tea and Chaos

"Would you pass the sausages round, please," Leila asked the wolf.

"All right," agreed the wolf. "But if it wasn't your party, I'd eat the lot and you too."

"Don't be silly," said Leila.

"Don't *you* be silly," said the

wolf. "Just remember what nearly happened to Red Riding Hood."

Everyone ate lots of food. The dragon took a fancy to the cheese and pineapple cubes and ate the lot in one go. The ugly sisters cried until they were offered an extra cake each. The last thing was a huge box of chocolates that Leila's Uncle Fred had sent her. She passed them round. After the forty thieves had all had one, and the wolf, and the ugly sisters, there was only one left.

"*I* ought to have it," said the giant. "*He* ate all the cheese and pineapple cubes."

"I want a chocolate," said the dragon, with a tear running down his face.

"You be quiet," said the giant, "or
I'll hit you!"

"If you hit me," said the dragon,
"I'll burn your beard!"

"Now *be quiet* you two," said
Leila. "This is a *nice* party."

Then one of the forty thieves
looked out of the window.

"Hey, fellas," he said. "all the
windows around here are open.
They will be easy to climb into.
On your way, lads."

"Bye, Leila," they said.
"See you later. We've just got

some work to do."

And off they went. Leila looked
out of the window and saw each
one of them disappear into a
different house in the street.

"Oh dear," said Leila. "They are
going to rob all the people in the
street. What shall I do?"

"That's *your* problem," said the wolf, laughing. "Now I think I can hear the children coming out of school. I do still feel a bit hungry. See you soon. Bye for now." And off *he* went.

"I'm beginning to wonder if
this party was a good idea," said
Leila.

"Bit late to think of that now," said the giant and then he sniffed.

"Fee, fi, fo, fum,
I smell the blood of an
    Englishman,
Be he alive or be he dead,
I'll grind his bones to
    make my bread."

And he stood up and walked off shouting and stamping his feet.

"This is *awful*," said Leila. "It's getting worse and worse. Dragon, what can I do?"

There was a sound of bells in the distance.

"Ah! A fire-engine," said the

dragon, sitting up. "I *love* that sound. I want lots and lots of fire-engines to come. I'll be off for a while and start a few little fires. Nothing for you to worry about, dear. Back in a bit."

Leila felt sick. Only the two ugly
sisters were left.

"Did you see that?" she said.
"They've all gone off to start
fires and rob people and eat
children."

"Well, what did you expect?"
said the skinny sister. "Not a nice

class of person you invited to your party. You've got to expect bad behaviour from that sort."

"Quite," said the fat sister. "You should only have invited us girls and then we could have had a nice quiet little party. Yes, we could have dressed up nicely and . . ."

"Talking about dressing up," said her sister, "Leila's mother must have some nice clothes."

"I *bet* she has," said the fat sister. "And lots of make-up too. Come on, let's go and find her bedroom. Won't be long, dear. You just have a nice little sleep."

Leila buried her head under the duvet. She could hear lots of fire-engines and children screaming and the giant shouting:

"Fee, fi, fo, fum, I smell the blood of an Englishman."

And cries of, "Stop, thief!"

And the ugly sisters saying, "Try this lipstick, dear. I want that dress. Oh, look, now you've gone and torn it!"

"I'm never coming out from under this duvet," thought Leila. "Never, never, never."

Then she heard Mum's voice.

"Wake up, Leila."

"I'm not coming out," said Leila.

"Never, never, never!"

"Why ever not?" said Mum.

"'Cos they're trying on your clothes and make-up."

"What *do* you mean?" laughed Mum. "No one's trying on my clothes and make-up."

Leila peeped out from under her duvet.

"And the fires?"

"What fires?" asked her mother.

Leila came out a bit further.

"And what about the children coming home from school?"

"Well, what *about* the children coming home from school?" asked her mother.

Leila came right out.

"So what happened to all the thieves?" she asked.

Her mother laughed. "I think you've been having bad dreams."

"No I haven't," said Leila. "All the baddies came to my party and then they all went off to do bad things. I think they must have

seen you coming up the road and run off."

"Yes," said her mother. "I expect that's what did happen."

But as Leila looked up, she saw the glass slipper on the table. She smiled a secret smile and thought, "I really *did* have a magical monster party. It definitely wasn't just a dream."

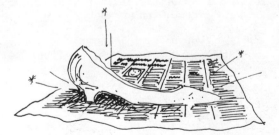

Barn Owl Books

THE PUBLISHING HOUSE DEVOTED ENTIRELY TO
THE REPRINTING OF CHILDREN'S BOOKS

RECENT TITLES

The Spiral Stair – Joan Aiken
Giraffe thieves are about! Arabel and her raven have to act fast

Your Guess is as Good as Mine – Bernard Ashley
Nicky gets into a stranger's car by mistake

Voyage – Adèle Geras
Story of four young Russians sailing to the US in 1904

Private – Keep Out! – Gwen Grant
Diary of the youngest of six in the 1940s

The Mustang Machine – Chris Powling
A magic bike sorts out the bullies

You're Thinking about Doughnuts – Michael Rosen
Frank is left alone in a scary museum at night

Jimmy Jelly – Jacqueline Wilson
A T.V. personality is confronted by his greatest fan